GW01087066

JAMES NEWMAN

MARK STEENSLAND

www.encyclopocalypse.com

For Rick Hautala

A SPECIAL INTRODUCTION TO THE SPECIAL

BRIAN KEENE

Be in this business twenty-plus years as I have, and sooner or later, you get to know everybody—and I do mean everybody. I keep my cell phone password-locked because if it was ever lost or stolen, Stephen King and Dean Koontz and John Carpenter would be getting prank phone calls from whomever had it.

If you think of the horror genre as a spider's web, as I often do, it's fascinating to sit back and watch how it's all interconnected, and how those seemingly disparate strands often make something special when they find each other.

James Newman and I go back to the very beginning. We met online around 1998 or so. And when I say online, I'm talking about the early days of the Internet, when social media hadn't been invented yet, and there were a grand total of five websites dedicated to horror fiction. Think about that for a moment. Five. Yes, James and I are old. Shut up. Mark Steensland and I don't go back that far (even though he's old like James and I). I first met him at a convention called Necon, in...I want to say 2008 or 2009, perhaps? And director B.

Harrison Smith is a homeboy who lives right across the Susquehanna River from me.

So...three individual creators, connected through the horror web. What happens when they join forces?

Something quite special. *The Special*, in fact.

Author Wesley Southard and I were very excited when we heard that not only was *The Special* being adapted into a film, but it was going to have its world premiere right here where we live in Central Pennsylvania. I was excited because James, Mark, and Harrison all deserved this moment and it makes me happy when people I like have a win. Wesley was excited because he's just about the biggest James Newman fan you'll ever meet.

We attended the premiere with our significant others, author Mary SanGiovanni and podcaster Katie Southard. Also with us were authors Kelli Owen and Robert Ford, and director Mike Lombardo (whom I produced a feature length film for and—in yet another example of the interconnected strands of the web, assisted with the special effects on *The Special*).

The film adaptation is pretty faithful to the original novella it was based upon—which you are reading right now (or will be after I stop rambling). Without spoilers, *The Special* is a wonderful slice of surreal horror — think Bentley Little or Edward Lee as directed by Peter Jackson during the *Dead Alive* and *Meet The Feebles* era. It's a deft blend of several overlapping sub-genres — extreme horror, psychological horror, sexual horror, and comedic horror. In lesser hands, the transition between these elements could have been jarring, but James and Mark handle them deftly, and Harrison translated them to the screen just as smartly. The story plays with questions of consent in a way that will make you uncomfortable — and that's what good horror should always do. But underneath it all is a dark and sobering meditation on addiction and sexual abuse.

And that's what any author wants, really. A number of my books and stories have been adapted for film over the years. Some of them have turned out great. Others lost the vision somewhere along the way. As an author, all you can do is shrug and cash the check, and if a reader gives you shit about the adaptation, you point to the book or the story and say, "It's still there, just the way you remember it." James and Mark should rest easy in this regard. It's obvious to me that a lot of care and thought and heart went into this adaptation of their work, and that's the type of partnership every creative wants in this business.

Because that type of creative synergy is something very special, indeed.

Brian Keene
somewhere along the banks of
the Susquehanna River, June, 2020

"(Can) one desire too much of a good thing?"

WILLIAM SHAKESPEARE, *AS YOU LIKE IT*

"Too much of a good thing can be wonderful!"

MAE WEST

"Whether you sniff it smoke it eat it or shove it up your ass the result is the same: addiction."

WILLIAM S. BURROUGHS

"ALL I'M SAYING IS, what's good for the goose is good for the gander."

"What does that even mean?"

"I'll tell you what it means." Mike finished off his beer in one swallow, slammed down the empty mug. "Once she stepped out on you, she wrote you a blank check to do the same. Unspoken rule."

"Is it?" Jerry's own beer sat untouched for the last few minutes. He was busy fidgeting with a bowl of peanuts.

"If it's not," said Mike, "it should be."

Jerry looked up at his friend with wet eyes. "How could she do this to me, Mike?"

Mike reached past him, plucked a peanut from the bowl. "You can't let her get away with it, Jerry. That's why you need to do this tonight. While you're still pissed off at the bitch."

"Hey, man, take it easy—"

"Sorry. I didn't mean to call her a bitch. But you and me, we've been pals for, what, going on twenty years? You just found out Lisa's been cheating on you. She's not my favorite person in the world right now."

"Ever heard that saying two wrongs don't make a right?"

"Sure, and whoever came up with that shit wasn't working eighty hours a week while his old lady was riding some other dude like a Harley on a bad piece of road. You need to stand up for yourself. She does it once and you don't hit back hard, she's gonna do it again. I've got another saying for you: drastic times call for drastic measures. If you do this, Lisa will think twice about cheating on you again. You set a precedent, save your marriage, and at the same time get to experience the most mind-blowing, out-of-this-

1

world orgasm you have ever known. Where's the problem?"

"I don't know, man. Even if I wanted to do this, it's not like women are throwing themselves at my feet. I'm thirty pounds overweight. Got more hair on my chest than on my head. And I've got this patch of eczema on my—"

"I don't want to hear about that. Why would I want to hear about that? Doesn't matter anyway. There is always opportunity, Jerry. And you don't have to worry about a thing. Mikey's got you covered."

"Okay. So who am I gonna do it with? Mort?"

"Nah. I hear he's a selfish lover."

"Forget it, Jer," the bartender said, without looking their way. He was a fat man with long white hair and a face pockmarked with old acne scars. The T-shirt stretched across his belly read "I DON'T NEED SEX, THE GOVERNMENT FUCKS ME EVERYDAY!" Until now his attention had been glued to a football game on the TV behind the bar. "Heard you give one hell of a hand job, but you ain't my type."

Jerry gave him a mock salute.

Across the room, a skinny twenty-something in a Charlotte Hornets jersey fed a dollar bill into the jukebox. The opening chords of Led Zeppelin's "Nobody's Fault But Mine" vibrated through the foundations of Mort's Hole-In-the-Wall. The guy returned to a rowdy table occupied by two of his friends and three attractive blondes. He said something to the others and they all cracked up as they looked over at Mike and Jerry.

"Remember when that was us?" Jerry said. "Making fun of the middle-aged stiffs in their suits and ties...didn't have a care in the world back then."

Mike scooped up his keys on their BMW fob. "That's it. I refuse to let you live like this. Pay the man. We can be there in ten if we don't hit any traffic."

"Where are you taking me, exactly?" Jerry dug through his wallet, tossed some bills down on the bar. He glanced around, as if afraid that someone might overhear: "It's not some kind of...whorehouse, is it?"

"You guessed it. There's a rusty Airstream in the woods off Exit 80 that's the answer to all your problems. None of the girls speak English, and maybe they got bad teeth, but you can rest assured they've had their shots! Would you trust your old buddy for once? It's not at all what you think."

"Fine." Jerry stood up from his stool, a bit unsteadily. "Screw it. Lead the way."

Mike slapped him on the back. "I promise you won't regret this."

"Let's just go. Before I change my mind."

The night was cool and bright. A full moon hung high in the sky like a gargantuan eye watching the men make their way to Mike's Beemer. The air smelled of diesel exhaust from the nearby overpass and the garbage overflowing in the bins out back of the bar. The sign in front of the place ("TAVERN OPEN DAILY 6-2") flickered and buzzed like something slowly succumbing to a serious injury. Mort's Hole-In-the-Wall was a dump, in the kindest of words. The booze tasted like watered-down piss, the bathrooms were so disgusting it was safer to go outside, and although it was located in a section of the city that folks like Mike and Jerry normally tried to avoid, it was the sort of joint they could haunt after work without worrying that they might bump into some asshole from the office.

As soon as their seatbelts were on, Mike started rifling through a pile of trash on the floorboard behind the passenger seat.

Jerry stared straight ahead, through the windshield. Across the road from Mort's Hole-In-the-Wall was a massive bridge abutment covered in graffiti. A scrawl of tall green letters declared "NINE-INCH NOLAN NEVER SAY DIE." That always made Jerry chuckle. He worked with a guy named Nolan. He often imagined the prissy little shit sneaking down here under cover of night, tagging the bridge with his wishful *nom de guerre*.

But tonight he was in no laughing mood. "What the hell are you looking for?"

"This should do the trick. Put this on."

Mike handed him a brown paper bag. It was from a local fast-food restaurant.

"You're kidding, right?" said Jerry.

"Nope."

"Why the hell would I wanna do that?"

"Let's just say...after one taste of what you are about to experience, you'll be dying to go back for more. It's that good, Jerry. But I can't let that happen. I'd never be able to live with myself if you got in too deep."

"You know, this whole thing is starting to sound a little sinister. Like I'm gonna end up tied to a chair while some German guy with a tray full of torture tools demands I tell him stuff I don't even know."

"Ha! I love that movie. *Is it safe?*"

"I'm kidding," Jerry said, "but I'm not."

"I'm doing this for your own good," Mike said. "Call it a...preventative measure."

Jerry just sat there, staring down at the bag in his hand. "You'll thank me later," Mike said.

"This is ridiculous."

"Think about Lisa...bucking and grinding against some other douchebag...while you're busting your ass trying to pay for that second mortgage you never wanted in the first place."

Jerry slid the bag over his head. It smelled like chili cheese fries.

"You won't regret this," Mike said.

He started the car, revved the engine, and pulled out of the lot.

———

A mile or so from their destination they stopped at a traffic light. Its ruby glow shined on the car like blood splashed across the Beemer's hood. Mike's fingers tapped a rhythm on the steering wheel as he waited. To his left sat a pawnshop with bars on its windows. Two mangy-looking cats were engaged in coitus on the shop's front steps.

"You should see these two cats going at it," he said. "It's hilarious."

"Would if I could," Jerry's muffled voice said from inside the bag.

A car pulled up beside them. A late-model Mustang. "Can't Feel My Face" by The Weeknd blasted from the stereo. A muscular blond surfer type wearing a mesh shirt sat behind the wheel. The guy in the passenger seat could have been his identical twin, except the latter was so cool he wore his sunglasses at night. A third man with his hair braided into cornrows lay sprawled in the backseat, puffing on one of those vaping thingamajigs.

"I know how you feel, bro!" the driver shouted Mike's way. "I had to do the same thing with my last piece of tail!"

The others roared with laughter.

Mike couldn't help it; he laughed along with them. "Oh, for fuck's sake," said Jerry.

The Mustang peeled out, took off down the street.

Jerry slowly turned his head toward Mike. "I'm guessing the light is green now. Please go."

Mike gassed it and they headed deeper into the city.

"Here we are. Welcome to Madame Zhora's."

"You told me it wasn't a whorehouse."

"She's not that kind of madam. You can take the bag off now."

Jerry ripped it off. His face was shiny with sweat and maybe a hint of leftover fast-food grease.

Mike brought the Beemer to a smooth stop in front of a two-story house. Although he had been here before, six months had passed since the last time he had used Madame Zhora's services (moderation, that's the key, just like he'd warned Jerry) and he was once again struck by how unassuming the house appeared.

One could never have imagined what pleasures awaited inside. Its mustard-yellow paint was peeling all over. Half of the shingles were missing from its roof. A green neon sign blinked in one of its ground-floor windows: "PSYCHIC." Parked to the right of the house was a shiny black Ford F150.

Jerry said, "A fortune-teller? Seriously, man? You know I don't believe in this crap. One of these cons took my grandma for everything she had when I was growing up. And besides, what's some stupid palm-reader got to do with Lisa cheating on—"

"It'll all be clear in a matter of minutes." Mike rolled up the windows, killed the ignition. "Remember what I said about trusting me?"

"This is crazy."

Mike climbed out of the car and started walking toward the house.

Jerry got out too but just stood there by the Beemer, chewing at his bottom lip.

Mike used the key-fob to lock the doors. The vehicle beeped twice in reply. "Are you coming, or do I have to drag you inside?"

Reluctantly, Jerry followed. "I'm coming."

"Oh, yeah," said Mike. "You're gonna be. You have no idea."

The foyer was uncomfortably warm. It was a small room with burgundy walls and a hardwood floor. Atop an end-table sat an expensive-looking lamp and a potpourri bowl shaped like a tiny witch's cauldron. On the opposite wall hung a large oil painting, a reproduction of Raphael's Three Graces. A curtain of multicolored beads separated the foyer from a dimly-lit hallway. From somewhere at the rear of the house came the sound of someone watching television; a man and woman were arguing in a foreign language to the delight of a studio audience.

On the wall to the left of the bead curtain was a

black button. A sign was taped above the button, black marker on a sheet of paper that had gone yellow with age: "RING FOR SERVICE," it read, and in smaller print beneath that, "CASH ONLY."

Mike pushed the button, then winked at Jerry, as if to say:

You have no idea what's in store for you....

Jerry rolled his eyes.

A minute passed, maybe more. Mike hummed the Zeppelin tune that had been playing at the bar. Jerry shifted his weight from one foot to the other, stared down at his palms as they waited. Was that old scar from a childhood skateboarding accident the cause of all his problems? Did his severed love-line have something to do with Lisa spreading her legs for another man? He shook his head. Didn't know his love-line from his happy trail. He couldn't believe that Mike would be gullible enough to fall for crap like this....

The bead curtain parted then, with a sound like hundreds of finger bones clacking together in anticipation of something momentous, and Madame Zhora made her appearance.

She was a hunched old woman with a tiny mouth and a sharp, birdlike nose. Her eyes were two glistening sapphires set deep within her skull. Her wrinkled face reminded Jerry of an apple that had been half-eaten then left to dry out in the sun. She wore a long, flowing dress the color of dried blood. Her wiry gray hair was barely contained by a green babushka.

"Madame Zhora?" said Mike.

"I am Madame Zhora," the old woman said in a thick Russian accent. "But you know this. You have been here before."

"Right," said Mike. "Madame, this is Jerry."

She looked Jerry up and down with her vibrant blue eyes.

Didn't seem impressed.

"We're here for the Special," Mike said.

Jerry shot him a questioning look. Mike ignored it.

Madame Zhora straightened slightly. Something cracked inside of her as she did so. "Both of you?" she said. "That will cost you." She thought about it for a moment. "Three times as much."

"Eww, no." Mike gave an awkward laugh. "Just my buddy here."

The old woman closed her eyes. Tilted her head toward the ceiling. Her nostrils flared. Her lips moved as if in prayer.

Jerry whispered to Mike, "Um, what's she doing?"

"I don't know," Mike replied. "She does this every time. All you need to worry about, my friend, is that you are about to have the best sex you've ever had."

"With her?"

Mike gave a snort of laughter. "Of course not."

Madame Zhora's eyes blinked open. She threw back her head and cackled madly, "You do not find me attractive? You should be so lucky!"

Jerry swallowed a lump in his throat, stared down at his feet. Mike chuckled. "We didn't mean to offend you, Madame."

"Did not offend." The old woman stopped laughing. "As long as you have money."

She stepped forward, snapped her fingers in Jerry's face. She opened her wrinkled fist, like some exotic flower slowly spreading its petals.

"Oh," said Mike. "This is my treat."

He laid four twenty-dollar bills in her palm.

Madame Zhora looked at the money, shook her head. "Is one hundred dollars now."

"Since when?" said Mike.

"Since last time you were here."

"You drive a hard bargain." Mike slid his wallet from his back pocket, pulled out another twenty. He winked at Jerry again as he handed over the bill. "But my buddy here, he's worth every penny."

Madame Zhora closed her fist, slid the cash into her blouse. "You," she said then, pointing a long, bony finger at Jerry.

"Follow me." To Mike she said, "You wait here."

"Of course," said Mike.

She disappeared through the curtain of beads. Jerry looked at Mike.

"Have fun," Mike said. "Hurry along now."

She led him upstairs. The old woman made no sound as she moved, but Jerry was self-consciously aware of every step he took up the stairs. Each one creaked beneath his weight, as if mocking him for whatever he was about to do.

At the top of the staircase they came to a short hallway. Hideous shag carpeting the color of urine led to three blood-red doors at the end of the hall.

The old woman stopped at the first door. She reached into her blouse, pulled out a key on a string. Unlocked the door with it.

"Come," she said.

Tentatively, Jerry followed her into the room.

She turned on the light, then left him alone without another word, closing the door behind her.

The room had no other doors, no windows. It smelled of lilac air freshener. Against the far wall was a sagging double bed. On the nightstand to the left of the bed was a pink Kleenex dispenser shaped like a valentine, beneath a lamp with a silver shade. At the foot of the bed, on a low, trapezoid-shaped end-table, sat an odd black cube—some sort of box.

Jerry heard a faint squishing sound, not unlike the sound an earthworm might make as it burrows through the soil, if such a sound were audible to the human ear. It was an alien noise, somehow obscene —although he didn't know why that word immediately came to mind—and it sent a chill down his spine. He was struck by the disquieting feeling that he was not alone in the room. But there was only his shadow on the wall.

He heard the sound again. Goosebumps prickled his forearms.

It was coming from that cube on the table at the foot of the bed.

He stepped forward for a closer look.

The box measured perhaps twelve inches square. It was constructed from good, solid wood— pine, most likely, but Jerry was no carpenter—and was painted black as night with a matte lacquer finish. Its lid had been padlocked shut. The lock was small but sturdy and painted the same deep black as the box itself, as were the hinges along its backside. In the front of the box was a round hole about twice the size a golf ball. A thin strip of green plastic was stuck to the box directly above the hole. It was from one of those cheap handheld label-makers. Four words embossed upon it in bold white letters told Jerry what he was supposed to do:

STICK IT IN HERE

"Oh, give me a fucking break."

Jerry glanced around the room, almost expecting to see the blinking red eye of a camera hidden behind the A/C vent in the corner. He tried to recall if he had ever heard of an X-rated version of *Candid Camera*, something that would make him the butt of a pornographic prank to the delight of perverts all over cyberspace....

He yanked out his cellphone, sent Mike a text message:

U MUST THINK IM STUPID

Mike replied a few seconds later:

lol...you found it

Jerry shot back with:

SORRY BUT SHE DOESNT DO
MUCH FOR ME.

Mike replied:

lmao!!!!! just do what it says!

Jerry crouched down in front of the box. Felt a wave of dizziness wash over him. Mike often called him a lightweight, said he couldn't handle his beer, and he was right.

He stared into the hole. Could see only darkness inside. He touched the sides of the hole with his middle finger. From the feel of it, the box was hollow.

He sent Mike another text message:

WHAT THE HELL IS IT? ONE OF THOSE GLORY HOLES OR SOMETHING???

Mike replied a minute later:

or something ;)

Jerry wiped his sweaty hands on his pants.

His phone buzzed again as another message came through:

hurry up, stud......getting late

He slid his phone into his back pocket. Took a

deep breath. Thought of Lisa writhing under another man, someone much younger and fitter than himself....

This wasn't the same. Wasn't as bad as Lisa's infidelity. If he went through with it, he was pretty sure he could live with himself after the deed was done. For that matter, does this even count as cheating? It's just a fucking box. That made a high-pitched burble of nervous laughter slip out of him: a fucking box.

Jerry unzipped his pants.

From downstairs in the foyer, Mike heard Jerry scream. It was a long, wavering shriek that sounded as if his friend was being ripped to pieces.

He smiled, even as he felt a twinge of unease. He hoped he hadn't made a mistake by bringing Jerry here.

It'll be fine, he reassured himself. Jerry's got a good head on his shoulders.

"Yeah," he said. "I'm sure it will be fine."

Madame Zhora returned to the foyer with a teacup in her hand. "It is finished," she said. "Gather your friend. Leave. I am old and I must have my sleep."

"Sure thing," said Mike. "So, I should...?"

"First door on left." She took a long sip at her tea before offering Mike a crooked grin. "But I am sure you remember."

He knocked on the door. "Jerry?" No answer.

Mike held his ear to the door. Noticed as he did so that the wood around the jamb was marred by several thin, splintery gouges; there were tiny scratches on the doorknob too, around the keyhole, as if someone had tried to break inside the room at some point and Madame Zhora had never gotten around to repairing the damage.

"Jerry!" He knocked again. "Time to go, loverboy." He opened the door and stepped into the room.

Jerry lay on his stomach. His pants were around his ankles, his dimpled white ass nearly glowing in the light from the bedside lamp. At first glance, the way he was sprawled there beneath the box, he looked like a religious zealot lying prone before an apathetic god.

"Is he breathing?"

Mike turned to find Madame Zhora standing behind him. The expression on her face was that of a mischievous child who is privy to a secret that no one else knows.

Mike bent, shook Jerry by the shoulder. "Wake up, man. We gotta hit the road."

Jerry groaned, said something that sounded like, "Never felt anything like that "

"It's alive," Mike said.

"You must leave now," Madame Zhora said.

"Got it," said Mike. "We're going."

He nudged Jerry again. Got no response this time. Tried to lift him but lost his grip on his friend's sweaty shoulders and Jerry fell back onto the floor face-first.

"Shit."

"Ivan!" the old woman called out over her shoulder, followed by something in Russian.

"No need to call Ivan," said Mike. "I've got this. Just let me—" Heavy footsteps clomped up the stairs.

A man entered the room behind Madame Zhora. He looked like several boulders stacked on top of each other. He was so tall he was forced to duck to get through the doorway. He was bald, but with a reddish-brown beard that was large enough to smuggle an infant inside of it if he ever needed to do so. He wore a white tank top, black jeans, and heavy work boots. A tattoo on one of his massive biceps portrayed a gory rendering of a decapitated wolf's head.

"*Yest li problema zdes?*" His voice was deep, like something rumbling up from the bowels of the Earth.

"I*m pora ukhodit,*" the old woman replied.

"He's heavier than he looks," said Mike. "Just give me a minute, we'll be out of your hair and—"

"I have no hair," said Ivan.

Mike chuckled uneasily. The big man didn't crack a smile. "Cover him, *podonok*. We cannot carry him out like that."

"Right." Mike made a face as if he had just bitten into something sour as he pulled up Jerry's underwear and pants.

"You get his legs," said Ivan. "I get his arms."

They hefted Jerry between them and carried him from the room.

"I need raise, *tetka*." Ivan said over his shoulder. "You do not pay me enough for this."

The old woman cackled like that was the funniest thing she had ever heard.

"I pay you more than you deserve," she said, locking the door behind her with the key around her neck.

It was coming up on eleven by the time they pulled into Jerry's driveway. The house was dark. Mike knew from experience what that meant. The last woman he had lived with—an arrangement that barely lasted a year—liked to do the same thing when he stayed out too late with his friends. It was a way to let him know that she had long since gone to bed and he would hear all about it in the morning.

And that's exactly why I'm single, Mike thought.

By the headlights of his Beemer, Mike walked Jerry to his front door. A breeze tousled his friend's thinning hair. The air smelled of recently mown grass.

"Mike?" Jerry mumbled. "What happened in that room...was it real?"

"Told you it was incredible, didn't I?"

"What the hell was in that box?"

"I don't know," Mike said, "and I'm not sure I want to know. Do you?"

"No," Jerry said. "I guess not."

A dog barked in the distance. Crickets chirped in the bushes between Jerry's yard and his next-door neighbor's.

"Now remember what you gotta do," Mike said as they climbed the steps up to Jerry's front porch. "You gotta rub it in Lisa's face. Tell her this is what happens when she betrays your trust. Make sure she knows you just had the best sex of your life."

"With a box," Jerry said.

"Well, you might want to leave that part out." Jerry stumbled. Mike caught him.

"My God, Mike...I can't even feel my legs. That was more than an orgasm, man. That was—"

"I know, buddy. I know."

The porch light flicked on. The front door creaked open. "Oh, shit," Jerry giggled. "I'm in trouble."

"Look what the cat dragged in," said Lisa.

Jerry's wife was a pretty brunette with a sharp jaw and a dark complexion. She was tall and slender, Jerry's opposite in every way. She wore a green bathrobe with pink pajamas underneath. In one hand she held a thick paperback novel. Perhaps she had waited up for him after all.

"Where in the world have you been?" she asked her husband as he clomped across the porch.

"Where does it look like?"

"Out drinking with Mike again. On a work night, which I'm sure you'll regret in the morning."

"Maybe," said Jerry. "Maybe not."

"Have a good time?"

"I had a great time," Jerry replied.

"Okay," Mike said, once they were inside and Jerry was safe on the sofa. "I'm gonna take off. He's all yours, Lisa."

"Thanks, Mike," Jerry said.

"Yeah," Lisa said dryly. "Thanks so much, Mike."

"Anytime." Mike patted his friend on the shoulder. "Sleep well, remember what I said, and I'll see you in the morning, stud."

Mike sat in his cubicle at Lakeshore Securities the next morning, waiting impatiently for his PC to download the latest virus definitions. This was going to take a while. You'd think the nerds in I.T. would be smart enough to schedule this crap on the weekend, when everyone wasn't scrambling to wrap things up on the last day of the fiscal quarter....

He thought about hitting the breakroom to refill his coffee mug. Maybe he would drop by the receptionist's desk on his way back, flirt with her for a while. Trudy was dumber than a box of paperclips but he could stare at that rack all day long.

He glanced back at his monitor, saw that the progress bar was only 1% closer to completion since the last time he had looked. He sighed.

Shortly before ten a.m., Jerry walked by. "Whoa," Mike said. "Jerry! Hey."

Jerry's hair was messy and unwashed, his complexion pale. His tie was crooked and his shirt was untucked on one side. He wore a pair of cheap sunglasses. They still had a price tag stuck to the temple, from the convenience store down the block.

"Whatcha need, Mike?" Jerry said. "I just got here. Tucker's gonna chew me a new asshole if I don't have that H.M.C. report on his desk by End of Da—"

"You're screwed then," Mike said. "Nobody's getting any work done for a while."

He told Jerry about the virus definitions. "Perfect," Jerry groaned.

"No offense, man, but you look like hell," Mike said. "We didn't drink that much."

"I did," Jerry said. "Tied one on after you dropped me off. Drank 'til I blacked out."

Mike stood, pulled Jerry into his cubicle. Sat him down in the empty chair by his desk. He noticed his friend smelled like sweat and Old Spice. Mostly sweat.

"Did you tell Lisa about last night?"

JAMES NEWMAN & MARK STEENSLAND

Jerry shook his head. Covered his mouth with his fist to stifle a belch.

"What? Why not?"

"You got any aspirin?"

Mike rummaged through his desk. Found a bottle. He offered it to Jerry, who shook out three pills and dry-swallowed them with a grimace.

"Why didn't you tell her?" Mike asked him again.

"Because I was wrong."

"What?"

"I was wrong, Mike. It was all a big mistake. That guy I saw at the house? The one I thought she was having an affair with? He was a sales clerk from the John Deere dealership. Turns out she's buying me a lawnmower for my birthday. It was supposed to be a surprise. He was just a sales clerk, Mike!"

"Aww, damn," said Mike.

"Do you know what this means?" Jerry exclaimed. "It means I'm the cheater, Mike! I'm a scumbag cheater!"

Mike peeked over his cubicle half-wall. Saw at least three of his fellow employees doing the same, frowning in his direction. His department head was one of them.

"Jerry, you need to keep your voice down." Jerry held his head in his hands.

"So you didn't tell her anything," Mike said.

"Hell, no."

"Good. So you can forget all about it. Pretend it never happened. Tell yourself it was nothing but a wet dream."

Jerry looked up at him with bloodshot eyes. "That's just it. I can't pretend it never happened. I can't get it out of my head."

"You will. Just give it a couple of days, kiss Lisa's ass, and everything will return to normal. You'll see—"

"No," Jerry said. "You don't understand."

"I guess I don't."

"You have to tell me where it is. Madame Zhora's place."

"Not gonna happen. I never should have taken you there in the first place."

"But you did, didn't you?" Jerry said. "You did take me there. And whatever happens next, it's all your fault."

Jerry flopped down into his chair with a sigh. He took off his sunglasses, tossed them onto his desk. Rubbed at his tired eyes, but then put the glasses back on after a minute or so. The overhead fluorescents were too much.

He spent the next few minutes checking his e-mails. Tried to type a reply to one, but he stopped in mid-sentence, unable to concentrate.

He opened a drawer in his desk. Took out a phonebook.

Flipped through to the yellow pages.

He looked up "FORTUNE TELLERS."

There was only one entry under that category. It was a quarter-page ad for a person who called herself "Mystic Wanda." Under her logo was a badly-drawn crystal ball with two long nailed feminine hands hovering over it.

Jerry ripped the page from the phonebook.

"If anyone asks," he told the receptionist on his way out, "I took an early lunch."

She glanced at the clock on the wall. It was barely half past ten.

She shrugged, before returning her attention to the celebrity gossip website on her computer.

———

Mystic Wanda's place was located in a strip mall downtown, between a consignment shop and a Domino's Pizza. A large neon sign shaped like a hand hung in one window, giving off a bright purple glow even in broad daylight. In the center of its palm were the words "PAST PRESENT FUTURE."

Jerry hurried inside.

The only light in her shop came from six electric candles, flickering in batwing-shaped sconces on the walls. In the middle of the room sat a small table with a wicker chair on either side of it. A pretty young woman with dark skin and curly black hair occupied the chair facing Jerry; a pile of Tarot cards lay in front of her, but she was busy playing with her iPhone. She wore a shimmering red-and-silver blouse and a long denim skirt. Faintly, from a single speaker installed in a corner of the room, John Lennon sang about how cold turkey had him on the run.

"Please." Mystic Wanda put her phone away and motioned toward the empty chair across from her. "Sit."

"I'm on my lunch break," Jerry said. "I don't have long. And I didn't come here for a reading. I need you to tell me where I can find Madame Zhora."

The fortune-teller gave him a puzzled look.

Jerry pulled out his wallet, tossed a ten-dollar

bill on the table. "I'm sure you keep tabs on the competition. She works out of her home. I don't know where that is. I need you to tell me."

Mystic Wanda looked down at the money, raised one eyebrow.

Jerry pulled out another ten, tossed it on the table. "That's all I've got."

"Vhat does zis...Madame Zhora...have zat I do not?" Her accent was atrocious, sounded like something she had heard in Dracula movies.

"Do you want the money or not?" Jerry asked her.

"I know of Madama Zhora," she said, "and I can tell you vhere she is."

"Great." Jerry glanced at his watch. "I'm waiting."

Jerry came to an awkward stop at the drive-through ATM. The Saab's tires squealed like a kicked puppy. A woman in a minivan was pulling away in front of him, taking her sweet time about it. She threw up a middle finger, cursed Jerry in her rearview mirror when he almost rear-ended her. But Jerry barely noticed.

He withdrew a hundred dollars.

Started to drive away, but then slid his card back into the machine.

He withdrew another two hundred. Just in case.

The door was locked. His pulse quickened. He started to breathe a little heavier. For a moment an image flashed through his mind of a wild-eyed junkie who just discovered that his only connection has dropped off the face of the Earth.

He knocked. Desperately. "Hello? Anybody home?"

"Am closed," said a muffled voice behind the door. "Come back later."

"I'm here for the Special," said Jerry.

"Am still closed," said the voice.

"I'll pay double."

The door opened, just a crack, and the old woman squinted out at him. "You were here last night. With other man."

Jerry glanced off toward the highway. "So what if I was."

"Is dangerous. Too much of good thing. You should wait a while. Or you will regret this later."

"I'll take my chances," Jerry said.

She held out her hand. Jerry noticed her nails had been painted since he saw her last. They were the color of shiny new pennies.

"The money," she said.

He slipped five crisp twenties into her palm. "You said you pay double."

"I did." He offered her a self-conscious grin along with the rest of the money. "It's worth it."

She slid the bills into her blouse before stepping aside to allow him entry. "I do not usually do this, you know."

"Do what?" Jerry said as he moved past her.

"Let people in when Ivan is gone."

"Yeah, well...business is business, right?"

"You try to take advantage of old woman, know that Ivan will be back soon."

"I promise you that's the last thing on my mind," Jerry said.

She looked him up and down for a moment,

suspiciously. Then she closed her eyes, tilted her head heavenward. Her nostrils flared. Her lips moved as if in prayer.

Her eyes fluttered open. "You know where to go. Do it fast and get out. I am trying to watch Oprah."

She didn't have to tell him twice. Jerry splashed through the bead curtain and raced up the stairs, already unbuckling his belt as he went.

———

Three minutes and forty-seven seconds later, Jerry collapsed on the bed, his face and arms bathed in sweat.

He stared up at the ceiling, wondered why he wasn't overcome with shame. He knew he should have been. He should have felt dirty. He thought of Lisa and her birthday surprise. But he felt nothing...only a burning desire to do this again. Soon.

He rose, grabbed his pants off the floor. Every muscle in his body ached as he dressed himself, as if he had just finished running a 5K instead of sticking his dick in a box.

He walked around the bed on weak legs to face the box again.

"What are you?"

He crouched, looked under the end-table. The box was secured to the trapezoid-shaped table by four small but sturdy brackets and wood screws. He pulled out his keys, turned on his LAKESHORE SECURITIES penlight and shined its beam into the hole, but he could see only blackness inside. A thin droplet of his ejaculate oozed from the bottom of the hole down the front of the box, like milky drool from a ravenous mouth. For a second Jerry thought about wiping it away—it would be the courteous thing to do—but he noticed that the valentine-shaped Kleenex dispenser on the nightstand was empty. It wasn't his problem anyway. The thought of some other man defiling the Special filled him with a strange sort of jealousy, not unlike the sick feeling that had come over him when he first suspected Lisa was cheating on him.

He shoved his keys back into his pocket, ran his fingers over the brackets and screws beneath the table.

He glanced around the room, searching for something that he might use to detach the box from the table. He had to know....

A knock at the door then. Madame Zhora asked from the other side, "You are finished, yes?"

Jerry shot to his feet. He ran to the door, opened it, pulled his remaining cash from his wallet. He shoved the money into her fist.

"One more time?"

"Is bad," Madame Zhora said. "I told you."

"You did. Like I said, I'll take my chances."

"After today you must wait at least one month. Cannot come back before. For your health."

"Sure. Whatever." Jerry slammed the door in her face. "For my health."

He whirled, pulled the table away from the bed with a grunt. Leaned it back so the box rested upon the footboard of the bed, with the table's rear legs on the floor. He climbed onto the bed, took a deep breath, then stepped onto the edge of the table with all his weight.

The box broke free with a loud CRACK...

...and Jerry heard something squeal.

"What the fuck?" He gasped, fell off of the bed. The door flew open.

"*Glupyy chelovek!*" Madame Zhora shouted at him. "What do you think you are doing?"

She bent, scooped the box into her arms as if consoling an injured pet.

Jerry jumped to his feet, grabbed one of the table legs.

He swung it, smashing Madame Zhora in the side of the head. The old woman hit the floor.

He struck her again.

The box tumbled from her grasp.

He stood over her, shaking. Slowly, his breathing returned to normal. He dropped the table leg.

He picked up the box and hurried out of the house.

He stopped at a gas station on his way—to where? *Don't even know what I plan to do when I get there*—and rushed inside to wash his face and hands in a filthy sink. He stared at himself for a long time in the scratched mirror. His forehead was shiny with sweat. His eyes were bloodshot. A line of graffito scrawled in red marker on the stall to his left seemed to mock him: "WERE ALL GOING TO HELL."

"Maybe," Jerry said. "Maybe."

He shared a sick chuckle with the man in the mirror.

He yanked a handful of paper towels from the dispenser then, scrubbed at a drop of dried blood on his neck until it was gone.

"Bathroom's for customers only, dude," the

pimply-faced kid behind the counter scolded him, as Jerry rushed through the store and back to his car.

Jerry ignored him.

He sat there in his Saab for a few minutes, his hands gripping the wheel as he stared at the black box on the passenger seat beside him.

"What are you?" he asked the box. It didn't answer.

"What comes next?"

He tore his eyes from the box and peered through the windshield.

Diagonally across the street from the gas station, a sign overlooked the highway. Beneath a faded picture of a plump orange sun peeking above a city skyline, it read:

SUNRISE MOTEL
$29.95/NITE WEEKLY RATES
HAVE YOUR NEXT AFFAIR HERE

Jerry started the car.

He turned on the light, pocketed the fob for Room 17. He peeked through the curtain, scanned the parking lot, making sure no one had seen him enter.

Carefully, as if handling something made of glass, he set the box upon the bed.

He stared down at it. Licked his lips. Touched himself through his pants.

He checked his watch, hissed a curse through his teeth. His lunch hour was nearly over.

For a moment he considered not going back to

work. But then he remembered the report his supervisor was waiting on. Tucker had strongly hinted that both of them might be looking for another job come morning, if that report wasn't on his desk by End of Day.

He cursed again.

Begrudgingly, Jerry opened the door, slipped the "DO NOT DISTURB" placard onto the handle, and got out of there for now.

"How long have you worked for...what was her real name again?"

Detective Jason Barnes flipped through his notepad. The lawman was older than he appeared, which frequently made folks underestimate him. He wore his bangs long and heavily gelled. He pushed his hair out of his eyes as he struggled to read his own handwriting. He was as tall but not nearly as muscular as the giant Russian who stood with him in the hallway, outside the perimeter of the crime scene.

"Grabinsky," Ivan replied, crossing his arms in front of his barrel chest. "Her name was Anya Grabinsky. I have worked here for one year."

"And what did you do for her?" the detective asked him.

"Security. Odd jobs. Anything she needed me to do around the place."

"Security." Barnes scribbled something on his pad. "Got it."

He didn't say anything for the next few seconds, just leaned against the wall and stared at the big man. It was a standard police tactic that worked every time: people don't like awkward silences, especially those who have something to hide. They will attempt to fill those silences. Allow them to do so, and eventually they will tell you something that you want to hear....

"She sent me to store for milk and bread," Ivan said. "She was not supposed to let anyone inside while I was gone."

"But she did," said Barnes. "And now...you should know that your boss is in bad shape, Mr. Marovich. I'm told it'll be a miracle if she pulls through."

As if on cue, two paramedics carried Madame Zhora out of the bedroom on a stretcher. One of them, a chubby black lady, barked at Detective Barnes and Ivan to make a hole. The old woman was unconscious but alive, breathing steadily with the aid of an oxygen mask.

The men stepped aside to let them pass. They watched the paramedics until they were out of sight at the bottom of the stairs. Ivan sniffled softly.

Barnes looked back into the bedroom then. "You're sure nothing was stolen?"

"I am sure," Ivan said.

"Just a broken table," Barnes said. "Care to tell me what this room was used for?"

"Spare bedroom. For visitors from homeland."

"I see. So...fortune-telling, that's the extent of Mrs. Grabinsky's business? Nothing else going on in this house that I might need to know about?"

Ivan stared at him, as if unsure what he meant.

The detective reached into his suit-jacket, traded his notepad for a plastic EVIDENCE baggie. Inside was a small green strip of plastic. Embossed upon it were the words "STICK IT IN HERE."

"Don't suppose you'd know what this is?" Ivan shook his head.

30

The two men watched through the doorway as a slim female detective with a silvery buzz-cut slid on a pair of rubber gloves. She bent to inspect the weapon that had been used to assault Madame Zhora. The bloody end of the table leg was wrapped in plastic.

"And you have no idea who could have done this?" Detective Barnes asked Ivan. "Or why?"

"She is gypsy Russian Jew," Ivan replied. "She has many enemies."

Barnes's expression said, *I don't follow.*

"Skinheads. Palestinians. Republicans. How do you say: take your pick."

Barnes closed his notebook. Tried to stare the big man down.

He lost.

"We are finished here, yes?" Ivan said. "I have much work to do."

"What kind of work?" Detective Barnes said.

"I also do her taxes."

"Better get on it," said Barnes. "April 15th's the day after tomorrow."

This time he won their staring contest. The big man stomped away, leaving the handsome young detective to his crime scene.

———

Jerry sat at his computer, trying to catch up. Easier said than done. All he could think about was the Special, waiting for him back at the motel....

Mike stepped into his cubicle at some point, said his name three times before Jerry looked up from hunting-and-pecking at his keyboard.

"Earth to Jerry."

"I'm here," Jerry said, without a hint of humor.

"I dropped by earlier to ask if you wanted to hit Chipotle for lunch. Trudy said you'd already been gone for an hour-and-a-half."

"I felt like being alone," Jerry said.

Mike moved some papers out of the chair next to Jerry's desk, made himself comfortable. "Was that all, man?"

"Uh-huh."

"No hard feelings, then? About last night?"

"Forgotten already. Isn't that what you said I should do?"

"Yeah."

"So that's what I'm doing. I'm pretending it never happened. I've got to put things right with Lisa. And in a week or so, everything will be back to normal."

Mike frowned. He couldn't help thinking that his friend's words sounded rehearsed, as if he were reading from a script that had been prepared ahead of time.

He gave Jerry a light punch on the shoulder. "Well, I can't tell you how glad I am to hear you say that. Wanna stop by Mort's on the way home? Two-Dollar-Tequila-Shot Tuesday. My treat."

"Maybe tomorrow," Jerry said. "I've already made reservations for dinner at P.F. Changs."

"You hate that place," Mike said.

"Lisa loves it."

"Right. Okay. Good. Maybe tomorrow, then?"

But Jerry had returned to his work and was no longer paying him any attention.

Mike sat at the bar by himself, deep in thought. "Man In a Box" by Alice In Chains thundered from the juke.

He flinched when Mort snatched his empty glass from in front of him.

"Mark my words," said the bartender. "One of these days, I'm rolling that damn thing out to the freeway, gonna replace it with one that plays nothing but Willie and Waylon. Punks come in here, all they wanna hear is this headbangin' shit."

Mike usually got a kick out of Mort's perpetually sour mood. It was part of what he loved about this place—you never knew what the crotchety old bastard was gonna say next or who/what he had decided to hate this week (tonight the slogan on his T-shirt read "ZIP IT, HIPPIE! NOBODY CARES ABOUT YOUR PROTEST"). But this time Mike barely heard Mort's commentary.

"Where's your drinking buddy, by the way? Thought you two were attached at the hip."

"He's out with his wife."

"Good for him, I guess. She prettier than you?"

"She is," Mike said, without really listening.

"Think you'll ever get hitched, Mikey?"

"Screw that. Married life ain't for me."

"Same," said Mort. "Too bad it took me three times to figure that out. Hey, I gotta step in the back for a minute. You want another Modelo?"

Mike shook his head. Threw some money on the bar and got up to leave.

He pulled to a stop in front of Madame Zhora's place.

The neon "PSYCHIC" sign in the window was dark. And there was a new sign in the other ground-floor window, a sloppy, hand-painted thing on a piece of battered cardboard: "CLOSED UNTIL FURTHER NOTICE."

Mike frowned.

The F150 was parked beside the house. Ivan was home, at least.

Mike sat there for a long moment, watching a crow nibble at something dead in Madame Zhora's front yard, before he pulled away from the curb and drove on toward home.

Jerry collapsed on the bed. His body tingled from head to toe. No drug could compare to the euphoria that washed over him when he used the Special. Every time felt like his first time all over again, but infinitely more amazing (that experienced older girl who had stolen his virginity at Bible camp the summer of his sixteenth year could have learned a lot from the Special). It was as if every molecule in his body had been torn apart then reassembled into something new, something superhuman, something indestructible.

"Fucking out of this world," he said, breathlessly, reaching out to run one sweaty fingertip along the box's backside.

After a while, when his heart rate had returned to normal and his juices had cooled upon his thigh, he got up to get dressed. His motel room was dark save for a thin shaft of bluish moonlight that slipped inside through a gap in the curtains. He moved the box from the bed to the closet, gently set it down on the floor next to an umbrella left behind by a previous guest.

He closed the closet door, stood there with his back against it for several minutes.

"You'll be safe here," he told the box. "I'll be back as soon as I can."

From inside the closet, he heard the muffled sound of something shifting...followed by a soft thump, like a footstep in the dead of night.

———

He crept into the house to find Lisa sitting on the sofa. On the muted television, a dreadlocked junkie with a teardrop tattoo on her face was cooking up a spoonful of heroin—the season premiere of one of their favorite crime shows. Lisa wore her pajamas and her reading glasses. She was pretending to be engrossed in a Dean Koontz paperback; she didn't look up right away when he walked in.

After a few seconds she creased a page to mark her place.

She set the book down and asked him, "How did it go?"

"How did what go?" Jerry said.

"The meeting with your department head?"

"Oh," he said. "It was fine. Boring. Thanks for asking."

"Jerry?"

"Yeah?"

She picked up the remote control from the arm of the sofa, turned off the television.

"It's late," she said. "Past nine. Were you really at work all this time?"

"What do you mean?" Jerry said.

"You weren't out drinking with Mike again, were you?"

He glanced down at his shoes, said, "No."

"I don't mind, honey," Lisa said. "I mean, I don't want to be a nag. But I worry about you. I know what your father went through, and that's what killed your—"

"I know what happened to Dad and Uncle Freddy," Jerry said. "You don't have to remind me."

"I just want to make sure your drinking doesn't become a problem, that's all."

"I don't feel well," he said. "I'm gonna take a shower then hit the sack." He leaned over, kissed her on the forehead. "Don't worry. My drinking's not a problem."

───────

He was almost done—thinking about the Special the whole time, pondering when he could get back to the box—when Lisa stepped into the shower with him.

He rinsed shampoo from his hair, opened his eyes. "Hey," he said with a start. "What are you doing?"

"What does it look like I'm doing? I thought I might help you feel better."

Her nipples were hard. She ran a fingernail down his stomach.

"I'm sorry, hon." He turned away from her, squeezed some body wash into his palm. "I don't think I can. I've had a headache all evening."

Lisa's laughter bounced off the walls of the shower stall.

"What's so funny?" said Jerry.

"This has to be the first time in history a man used that line."

He didn't get it.

"I have a headache?" she said.

"Oh."

She slapped him on the ass, teased him in a singsong voice as she exited the shower, "You don't know what you're missing!"

The next morning Lisa sat at the kitchen table, sipping from her INSTANT WRITER, JUST ADD COFFEE mug while she thumbed through the latest issue of a women's magazine that regularly featured her work. She had risen early, as she planned to get a jump on some editing before spending the rest of her day making last-minute preparations for Jerry's surprise birthday party.

She didn't hear him come into the room until he stole a bite of her toast. She looked up to see that he was fully dressed. There were dark bags under her husband's eyes, as if he hadn't slept well.

"I might be late again tonight," he told her.

"Leaving so early?" she said. "It's not even eight o' clock yet."

"That H.M.C. report got me behind on everything," Jerry explained. "I turned it in under deadline yesterday, but it should have been done a week ago. I'd rather cut into my mornings than my weekends."

"I'll see you tonight, then," Lisa sighed. "Late again." He left without his coffee. That was a first.

And...had he forgotten his briefcase?

She ran to the kitchen window, frowned as she

watched his Saab back out of their drive and head in the wrong direction.

Jerry pulled into the parking lot of Lakeshore Securities with a goofy grin on his face. He didn't even mind when he had to circle the lot twice before he found an empty space. Spending time with the Special made the extra hassle worthwhile.

His smile disappeared, though, as he killed the engine. His heart skipped a beat as he tried to remember: *Did I put the "DO NOT DISTURB" sign back on the door?*

I did. He nodded, climbed out of the car. *I'm sure I did.*

He entered the front lobby with a strut in his step.

The security guard looked up from his bank of closed-circuit monitors. "Morning, Mr. Harford."

"No, Earl," Jerry said. "Good morning. Good morning indeed, my friend."

The guard shook his head as he watched Jerry get on the elevator.

Somebody musta got laid last night....

As soon as Jerry walked into the company's office on the third floor, the receptionist made sure he knew: "You're late again."

He winked at her. "Time ain't nothing but a number, Trudy."

"What does that even mean?" she said.

"I have no idea."

Mike's phone rang shortly after nine a.m. It was an outside line. He sighed. Trudy was such an airhead. He had told her to hold his calls until after lunch.

He picked up. "Lakeshore Securities. Mike Adamson speaking."

"Mike? It's Lisa."

"Lisa?"

"Jerry's wife."

Mike's mouth suddenly felt very dry. "Lisa. Um...hey. How are you?"

"I'm sorry to bother you at work, Mike, but I was wondering if I could talk to you for a minute. It's about Jerry."

"Sure," said Mike. "What about him?"

"Does he seem like himself to you lately?"

"How do you mean?"

"I don't know. This probably sounds silly." He heard her take a deep breath on the other end of the line. "This morning, when he left for work, he went the wrong way."

"I'm not sure I follow."

She laughed, but it was obvious her heart wasn't in it. "If you did, you would have ended up somewhere other than the office. That's what I'm saying. He turns left to go to work. If he turns right, that would lead him toward the city. He turned right. Which makes me think he was lying to me when he said he was heading in to work early."

Mike didn't say anything. He knew that Jerry was the kind of guy who avoided O.T. if he could help it. Lately it would have been a stretch to say that he was here when he should have been....

"It sounds ridiculous when I say it out loud," she admitted. "I'm sure it's nothing. I just hoped maybe he'd told you something that he hasn't told me."

"Lisa," Mike said, "do you think something else is going on here?"

"He's not having an affair, is he, Mike?" Lisa said.

"God, no," Mike said. "I mean, if so, he hasn't told me about it."

"Do you think he would?"

Mike considered for a moment whether or not he should keep his mouth shut, then figured what the hell. "He thought you were the one who was messing around."

"Yeah," she said. "He was wrong."

"The birthday surprise," said Mike.

"The birthday surprise," said Lisa.

Neither of them spoke for a long, awkward moment.

"I know this sounds silly," Lisa finally said, "but would you do me a favor?"

"Sure."

"If you see or hear anything suspicious...will you let me know?"

"I can do that."

"I'd really appreciate it. I'm sure it's nothing."

"Yeah," Mike said. "It's probably nothing."

"Take care, Mike."

"You too, Lisa."

As soon as he hung up, a voice behind him said, "Was that my Lisa you were talking to?"

His heart leaped into his throat.

Jerry stood there with his arms crossed in front of his chest. Once again, his clothes were wrinkled. Once again, he wore a pair of cheap sunglasses. He smelled...fishy. Like a room in which strangers have sex with no strings attached.

"You scared the crap outta me, man," Mike said.

"Was that my Lisa?" Jerry asked him again.

"Yeah," Mike said. "As a matter of fact, it was. Know why she called me? She thinks you're screwing around on her."

"Hmm," said Jerry.

"Are you?"

"Am I what?"

"Screwing around on her. You can tell me."

"No," Jerry said, "I'm not." He looked right at Mike as he said it, but behind his dark glasses his eyes could have been anywhere. On Mike's Beers of the World calendar. Or the Rubik's cube atop his PC. Or peeking over the half-wall into the adjacent cubicle, down Kerri the intern's blouse.

"What the hell's going on?" Mike said. "I thought you took Lisa to dinner last night. Patched things up."

"Yeah, it didn't go so well." Jerry sniffled. "You know, this is all your fault."

"Come again?"

"You're the one who took me to Madame Zhora's."

"I made a mistake," Mike admitted. "I'm sorry. There, I said it. What else do you want from me, man?"

"For starters, stop talking to my wife behind my back."

"She called me, just so you know."

"So next time, you don't fucking answer."

And with that Jerry stormed off, his hands balled into pale, sweaty fists.

"Jerry, wait!" Mike shouted after him.

But when he saw their fellow employees watching, whispering among themselves, he slumped back into his chair with a red face.

Man, you really blew it. How did you ever think he could handle it?

Ivan Marovich sat in a windowless gray room that smelled of coffee and cigarettes. Detective Barnes faced him, a manila folder open on the table between them. Atop a small stack of papers and photographs of the crime scene was the evidence baggie with the "STICK IT IN HERE" label inside. A silvery-haired female detective who had introduced herself to the Russian as Detective Traynor stood behind Barnes, her back against the wall. One hand was buried in the hip pocket of her navy-blue pantsuit; the other brought a Virginia Slim to her lips every few seconds as if she were some automaton programmed to make the move now and then in order to mimic life. Even when she took a drag and smoke wafted up into her eyes, Traynor's stern expression never changed.

"You have found the *yazychnik* who did this, yes?" Ivan asked Detective Barnes.

"Not yet," the younger man replied.

"But you found fingerprints."

"We did." Barnes pushed his bangs out of his eyes. "Unfortunately, it doesn't work in real life like it does in the movies. Even the best latent print doesn't do us a damn bit of good if the man"—his partner cleared her throat and Barnes corrected himself—"or woman who left it behind doesn't have some kind of criminal or military record."

"Why did you ask me to come here?" Ivan grunted.

"Let me ask you a question, Mr. Marovich. Have you ever had something stuck in your teeth? Piece of popcorn, maybe. Stuck way back here." Barnes sneered, showed the big man his teeth, touching his middle finger to an almost vampire-sharp molar.

"You can't get it out no matter how hard you try. You pick at it, pick at it. No luck. Has that ever happened to you?"

"I have used dental floss since I was little boy," said the Russian.

Barnes heard Detective Traynor stifle an uncharacteristic laugh behind him.

He squared his shoulders. "Allow me to be blunt, then. Do you know what that means?"

Ivan looked down at the decapitated wolf's head tattoo on his bicep. He scratched at it. "I am listening."

"My partner and I, we don't like your attitude, comrade. We're thinking that you don't seem too concerned with catching whoever did this to Ms. Grabinsky. In fact, we think you might know more about what happened to the old woman than you've been tell—"

"I understand, Detective," Ivan interrupted him. "I am this something stuck in your tooth, yes? You want to get it out! Because it is making you insane."

"Exactly."

"Let me explain something to both of you," Ivan said. "I do not have much faith in man's justice. Police? *Nizhe sobak.* Useless to me. When I was child in Soviet Union, many of my family were put in prison for reasons that were not fair. And so I came to believe that those who do evil to others will face a higher justice."

"You think God will punish them?" Barnes scoffed.

"You Americans have saying: what goes around comes around. You know it?"

"I do," said Barnes.

"I believe the *podonok* who hurt Madame Zhora will get what he deserves. Anya's suffering will be

43

nothing compared to what is coming to the man who did this to her."

"You're sure it was a man?" Barnes picked up the evidence bag, made a show of fidgeting with it.

"Or woman," said Ivan, locking eyes with Detective Traynor.

———

The door to Room 18 stood open. A cleaning cart was parked in front of it. From inside the room came the sound of someone pushing a vacuum cleaner back and forth.

Jerry's Saab jerked to a stop near Room 17. He jumped out and jogged inside.

"Excuse me, sir?" The maid peeked out. She was a pretty Hispanic lady who barely stood as tall as her cart. "You are the guest in 17?"

Jerry paused, his hand on the door handle. "What's it look like?"

"You need housekeeping?"

Jerry held up the "DO NOT DISTURB" sign, showed it to her as if it were something she had never seen before. "That's why this is here," he said. "I don't want anything. I don't want you to change the bed. I don't want you to bring clean towels. You are not to come into this room for any reason. Do you understand?"

The maid nodded sheepishly.

Jerry hung the sign back on the handle with a hand that was visibly trembling. He shoved through the door, slammed it behind him. Locked the deadbolt and secured the chain.

The maid called him an asshole in her native language, then returned to her vacuuming.

He hefted the box onto the bed. Unzipped his pants. Closed his eyes and inserted his cock into the hole...

...and suddenly he winced in pain, pulling out. "Jesus!"

Jerry ran into the bathroom, turned on the light.

A bright pink rash covered his genitals. Every inch of his skin was enflamed down there—all over his balls, along the length of his drooping penis. Splotchy, dime-sized patches were visible beneath his pubic hair.

"What the hell?" he gasped.

He grabbed a washcloth, ran it under the cold tap. Gently patted his groin with it, hissing as he did so.

He returned to the bed. Picked up the box and peered into the hole. As always, he could see only darkness.

He set the box back down. Ran his fingers over the padlock on the lid.

He winced again, scratched himself. It burned. Was this what an STD felt like?

He lay back, let the frigid breeze from the A/C wash over his naked crotch, and thought, *This can't be good....*

Thirty minutes later, Jerry sat in the waiting room of the county health clinic. He thumbed through a copy of *Sports Illustrated* to pass the time, without really seeing the words and pictures in front of him. To his left, an old man sat dozing with his mouth open, his head resting on the shoulder of a purple haired teenager. To his right, a young mother was talking on her cellphone while trying to keep her two small children from tearing the place apart. The little girl sobbed as her brother twisted her baby doll's head around the wrong way and told her it was dead.

Jerry groaned, rubbed at his temples. *Thank God Lisa and I agreed that we didn't want rugrats of our own....*

"We'll do it some other time," the young mother told the person on the other end of the line. "I'm pretty sure Eddie has to work this weekend."

Shit. That reminds me. Jerry reached into his pocket, pulled out his phone. Called the office.

"Lakeshore Securities," the receptionist answered on the fourth ring. "How may I direct your call?"

"Trudy? Hi. It's Jerry Harford. I need you to tell Tucker I won't make it back in today. I'm really sick."

"What about your meeting with the big dog?" Trudy said. "Mr. Roth and the clients from H.M.C.?"

"See if Mike can take the meeting for me. Tucker trusts him. I'm actually at the doctor right now. Hopefully I can kick this crap by tomorrow and make it in bright and early."

"Sure," said Trudy. "I'll pass it along."

Jerry thanked her, hung up the phone to find one of the brats standing in front of him.

"My daddy has a gun," the kid told him. "That's nice," Jerry replied.

"Toby," said his mom, "leave the nice man alone."

A nurse opened the door then, leaned out with a clipboard in her hand. "Mr. Smith?"

"That's me." Jerry stood, quickly crossed the room.

"Follow me, please," said the nurse.

Jerry sat on the examination table, his balls in the doctor's liver-spotted hands. The doc was in his late sixties, with broad shoulders and thick glasses that made his eyes look freakishly huge. Beneath his lab coat he wore a teal tie with little Jacksonville Jaguars logos all over it. His nametag read ROBERT WEAVER, M.D.

"By chance," the doctor said, lifting Jerry's penis to inspect it from every angle, "have you and the missus been having more sex than usual?"

"No," Jerry said. "A lot less, in fact. I, uh...I think she might be going through the change." He tensed. "Ow! Take it easy, doc. It's tender down there."

"Apologies," the doctor said. "I have to ask...have you had sex with anyone other than your wife recently?"

"No," Jerry replied too quickly.

The old man raised one bushy white eyebrow. "You're sure about that?"

"Of course I'm sure," Jerry said. "You think I've been sleepwalking down to the street corner?"

"Hmm." The doctor cupped Jerry's scrotum again, looked down his nose at it like a jeweler inspecting precious stones that were marred with imperfections.

"What is it, doc?"

"I can't help you if you don't tell me the truth, Mr. Smith."

"I haven't had sex with anybody else," Jerry insisted. "That is the truth."

"Masturbating more frequently?"

Jerry made a farting noise out one side of his mouth.

The doctor blinked at him from behind his thick glasses with an expression that said, *Is something funny?*

"I can't remember the last time I jerked off," said Jerry.

The doctor nodded. He leaned back, removed his rubber gloves.

"So...what is it?" Jerry asked him. "What's wrong with me?"

"Let me put it this way," said Dr. Weaver. "Whatever it is that you and your penis have been doing, you need to stop. At least, you need to stop doing it so much. Take a break. I would suggest ten days, maybe more."

"Ten days?" said Jerry.

"Maybe more."

Jerry's shoulders slumped.

The physician pulled a pad from his breast pocket, scribbled something on it. "I'm writing you a scrip for an anti-inflammatory ointment. Rub it on the affected area twice a day. It should clear up your problem in a week or so."

"Great," Jerry said, in a tone that suggested it was anything but.

Lisa pulled up next to Jerry's Saab in the driveway. She glanced at the clock on the dash, was surprised to find him home at three in the afternoon. She hefted two grocery bags from the passenger seat and went inside.

"Jerry?" she called out, as she placed the bags on the kitchen table. "Honey?"

He was lying in bed. A heavy brown comforter covered every inch of him except for one bare foot.

She tickled the bottom of his foot, something he normally hated, but he was as still as a corpse.

"Jerry, baby, are you okay?"

She tugged the comforter down to his waist. He opened his eyes.

"Hey," she said. "What's wrong?"

"Started coming down with something over lunch," he croaked. "Feel like death."

"Oh, no." Lisa placed her hand on his forehead. "You don't seem to be running a fever."

"I'll be okay," he said, twisting away from her. He rolled over, palmed the tube of prescription ointment off of the nightstand and tucked it under his pillow. "Just let me rest, please?"

"Have you taken anything?" she asked him.

He replied with a noncommittal grunt.

"I'll leave you alone, then," she said. "I'll check in on you before I start dinner."

He listened as her footsteps receded down the hallway. Once she was out of earshot, Jerry pulled up his pajama shirt and checked the rash.

It had spread upward, almost to his belly button. It was darker, too, on his scrotum and around the base of his penis. It had turned from a pinkish sunburn shade to a harsher crimson purple, like a blood blister ready to pop.

He scratched at it. Vigorously.

The following morning Lisa awoke to find Jerry's side of the bed empty. She heard his electric razor buzzing in the bathroom.

With a mischievous grin, she slipped out of bed.

He stood over the sink, clad only in his bathrobe. He was whistling some upbeat tune as he finished up. He went silent when he closed the cabinet and spotted his wife in the mirror behind him.

"Someone's feeling better," she said. "And I see you decided to ditch the mountain man look you've had going for the last few days. I'm glad."

He laughed. "I am feeling better. It's amazing what a good night's sleep can do for a person."

"I know what else is good for a person," she said. "Will you show me yours if I show you mine?"

She opened her robe, let it drop to the floor. She was naked underneath. Jerry wasn't the only one who had shaved recently.

His reflection blinked at her.

She reached for the belt on his robe, tugged at it. The robe fell open in front.

He gasped and quickly covered himself. "Can't you see I just took a shower? Besides, I gotta get to work."

"No time for a quickie, even?"

"Sorry. After missing half a day, I'm more behind than ever now."

"Fine." She snatched her robe off the floor. "Whatever." Threw it on. "I give up."

She slammed the door on her way out.

Jerry barely noticed. He had other things on his mind.

He pulled out of the driveway and again turned to the right.

Toward the city.

As soon as his car was out of sight, the garage door rolled up and Lisa's Altima backed out. She still wore only her bathrobe.

She followed him. But not too close.

Jerry wasn't quite two miles from home when he made the tail in his rearview.

"You gotta be fucking kidding me."

He didn't try to shake her. Instead, he took an alternate route that would lead him to the office, albeit in twice the time it normally took him to get there. He stopped off at a Dunkin' Donuts on the way. Lisa knew how much he loved their Big N' Toasted sandwich. On his way out, bag in hand, he scanned his surroundings from behind his sunglasses and spotted his wife's Altima idling among the inventory of a used car dealership on the other side of the highway.

"You think you're so fucking smart," he said without moving his lips.

He hit the road again. Watched her merge with traffic to follow him four cars back.

In that moment he was pretty sure he hated her. Not because she had forced him to drive around all over the city to alleviate her suspicions. Not because this would make him late for work again. He hated his wife because, due to her desire to play Dickless Tracy, he was wasting valuable time that he could be spending with the Special.

He called her a name he had never called her

before, not in seventeen years of marriage, and drove a little faster.

Ten minutes later he pulled into the parking lot of Lakeshore Securities. Waited until he saw her pass on the highway.

When he was satisfied that his ruse had worked, he started the engine again and pulled out of the lot.

At the first stoplight he came to, he tossed his untouched Big N' Toasted to a homeless man on the median. The guy thanked him as if he had just won the lottery, assuring him that the Lord was watching and he'd just bought a few more jewels for his Heavenly crown, but Jerry's attention was focused on a nearby billboard. "ADDICTED? GET HELP TODAY," it read, above a 1-800 number and a photo of a tabletop littered with syringes, smoldering joints, pills, and piles of white powder.

The light turned green. The car behind him beeped its horn. Jerry drove on.

This time, when he slid his cock into the Special, nothing happened.

The soft, warm wetness that usually greeted him the instant he entered the box...it was gone.

"Oh, no," Jerry said.

Something was wrong. He felt a hot flash of panic. He pulled out. Crouched down and stuck his finger into the hole.

Nothing. As if it had been hollow all along. He picked up the box. Shook it.

"No, damn you! This isn't happening!"

He dropped the box onto the bed. Tugged on the padlock.

His heart raced as he pulled up his pants and grabbed his keys.

———

The sign in the front window of Amstutz Hardware read "WE'RE CLOSED: PLEASE COME AGAIN! (OPEN DAILY 9-6)."

Jerry checked his watch, cursed through clenched teeth.

They didn't open for another twenty minutes.

He paced back and forth. Sweat trickled down his forehead, burned in his eyes. He realized his hands were shaking like a man suffering from the D.T.'s. He started gnawing at his fingernails—a habit he had kicked at Lisa's urging not long after they had first started dating.

"Come on," he growled. The minutes ticked by.

Finally, it was nine o' clock. Jerry cupped his trembling hands around his eyes to peer through the glass, fumed for another three or four minutes until some fucker finally opened the door.

"Good morning, sir," the clerk said as Jerry barged into the store. He was a lanky college-age kid with a mop of dirty blond hair, a bucktoothed grin, and earlobes stretched out by heavy gauge plugs.

"Thought you opened at nine," Jerry mumbled.

The guy looked at his watch. "I've got nine on the dot, sir."

"Whatever," Jerry said. "I need to know where to find the...shit, I don't know what they're called." He mimed working a tool with two big handles, like an oversized pair of pliers. "You use 'em to cut locks."

"Bolt-cutters? Right this way, sir."

The guy led him to what he was looking for, stood aside while Jerry considered his options.

"Lose the key, did you? How big is the lock?"

Jerry held up his thumb and forefinger, about three inches apart.

The clerk selected a mid-sized pair off the rack. "This should do the trick. If not, just bring back your receipt, we'll be glad to swap them for whatever you need. Piece of cake."

Jerry scratched himself through his pants as he followed the guy to the front register.

The bolt-cutters sliced through the padlock on his first try. In his excitement, Jerry nearly dropped the tool on his foot. He carefully lifted the box's lid. It came up slowly, as if attached to something heavy inside, before refusing to budge any further.

He pulled harder. Heard something that sounded like several rubber bands snapping.

The lid rose, fell back...and for the first time he saw what was inside.

He recoiled. The temperature in the room seemed to drop ten degrees.

Stuffed into the box was a grotesque mass of pale blue tissue shot through with wormy black veins. As Jerry gawked at it, an image of a throbbing tumor came to mind...or one of those hideous blob fish...or the top of Darth Vader's disfigured skull, glimpsed without his helmet. A sick titter slipped out of him at that last mental picture. It resembled all of those things and none of them at the same time. He leaned down for a closer look. The thing was weak, probably dying, but alive. It twitched—once, twice—and Jerry could see inside of it the flutter of a slow, off rhythm pulse. He covered his mouth and nose with one hand. The thing stank like the sea, and of creatures that crawled from its briny depths to die upon the shore.

He turned the box upside-down, tried to shake it out onto the bed. It didn't budge.

He dug a hand into each side, attempted to pry it out. Easier said than done. It was jammed in there good.

But finally, it flopped onto the bed. It shuddered, sighed.

Jerry picked it up. It wasn't as heavy as it looked. Twelve, fifteen pounds at most. He carried it into the bathroom. Turned on the light.

The thing contracted in his grip, hissed in his ear. Jerry gasped, threw it into the bathtub.

It shrieked.

He flicked off the light. It went silent.

He drew a cup of cold water from the sink then and knelt next to the tub. He poured some water over the thing from the box.

It made a satisfied cooing sound. Twitched. Began to purr.

Jerry's guts roiled, even as he became aroused. "You like that, huh? All better now?"

He poured more water over it. Caressed it, as if kneading a woman's breast.

Gradually, the thing's milky flesh darkened to a healthier pinkish hue.

Jerry smiled. He grabbed a towel and used it to lift the thing out of the tub.

He carried it back to the bed, and was preparing to lie down beside it when his cellphone chimed in his pocket.

It was a message from Mike:

> DUDE.......where ARE u?
> Tucker's on the warpath!

"Oh, fuck Tucker," Jerry spat, but he quickly pulled up the number for the office.

When the receptionist answered, he rattled off what he had to say in one breath: "Trudy. Jerry Harford. I'm afraid I'm still not feeling well. The doctor put me on some antibiotics, but I'm gonna need another day to kick this thing. Could you let Tucker know, please?"

He sighed as he listened to her reply.

"Tell him I'd be there if I could," he said. "Don't wanna spread this crap to everybody else. What? No. You're mistaken. You didn't see my car out front this morning, Trudy. I've been at home, in bed, since I spoke to you yesterday afternoon. Of course I'm sure. Okay, then. Bye."

He hung up. Dropped his phone.

He undressed and became one with the Special for a while.

When he was finished, he swung his legs over the side of the bed. Looked down at himself.

The rash had spread up his stomach, halfway to his nipples.

It took him a while to find the tube of ointment in his pile of clothes, but when he did he squeezed everything left inside of it into his palm. He spread the cream all over his torso and groin. It was cold. Felt good.

Afterward, he looked over his shoulder at the thing and asked it, "What have you done to me?"

It flexed as if in reply, made a wet smacking sound like lips savoring something delicious.

Jerry scratched at an itchy spot on his left shoulder, hoped that he would be ready to go again sooner than later.

———

Two days later, Lisa was sorting through their mail while she ignored the latest episode of Dr. Phil on TV. Her jaw dropped when she opened the card statement.

"Oh, Jerry. "

She muted the television. Thumbed through the phone book. Dialed a number.

"Sunrise Motel," said a husky female voice on the other end of the line.

"Hello," Lisa said. "Could you please tell me if you had a guest there on...April 13th?"

"What's the name, ma'am?"

"Harford." She spelled it.

"Yes. Mr. Harford is still here, in fact. He's been renting by the week. Would you like me to connect you?"

"I beg your pardon? He's still there?"

"That's right. Room 17."

Lisa hung up.

———

Lisa ripped the "DO NOT DISTURB" sign from the handle and threw it on the ground.

"Bastard!" she cried, pounding on the door.

"Fuck off!" Jerry's muffled voice shouted from inside. "I told you I don't want my room cleaned!"

"And why not, Jerry? Doing something in there that you don't want anyone to see?"

"Oh, my God. Lisa...?"

"Open the door, Jerry."

"Lisa, please...just go away."

"Open this door right now, or I swear to God I'll scream rape at the top of my lungs."

"No!" Jerry said. "Don't do that! I'm coming."

He scooped the thing up from the bed and rushed into the bathroom. It plopped into the tub. He yanked the shower curtain closed.

As soon as he opened the door his wife stormed into the room.

She gagged. Covered her mouth. "Jesus, Jerry...what stinks in here?"

"I don't know." He closed the door behind her. "It's an old room, I guess."

"No. Something reeks. That's awful! Is it her?"

"Who?"

"The skank you've been sleeping with."

"I don't know what you're talking about."

"Are you kidding me? You're going to stand here and deny it even though I caught you red-handed, curled up in your little love nest? God, you're pathetic. Where is she?"

"There's nobody here, Lisa. I swear."

"She's hiding in the bathroom, isn't she?"

"Lisa, no!" Jerry said. "Don't go in there!"

She pushed the door open. Flipped on the light. The thing in the tub let out a birdlike squawk.

"What the hell?" Lisa pulled aside the shower curtain.

"Lisa, don't—"

She screamed.

The thing screamed back at her.

Lisa stumbled backwards. "Wh-what is that?" she babbled. "J-Jesus Christ, what is that?"

Jerry stepped into the room behind her. The bolt-cutters were in his hand.

He swung them down with all his strength, and Lisa's forehead split open with a grisly crack.

He fell upon her, hit her again and again. Blood speckled his face and arms.

All the while, the thing in the bathtub squealed with delight.

Finally, Jerry collapsed beside his wife's corpse.

The thing sighed softly. As if it, too, was overcome with fatigue.

———

The sun was hot on the back of his neck as he rifled through the trunk of his Saab. He shoved aside a tire iron, a jug of motor oil, an old flannel shirt, and a ratchet set he had borrowed from a neighbor over a year ago. At last, he found what he was looking for: bungee cords.

He ran back into the room, the cords trailing behind him like demonic tails. He wasted no time wrapping Lisa's corpse in the blankets he ripped from the bed. He used the cords to cinch the whole thing tightly shut, like a giant burrito.

Once that was done he wiped down the bathroom. He grabbed a pair of plastic laundry bags out of the closet, threw the blood-soaked towels into one of them. He slid the Special into the other.

"Just for now," Jerry promised it. "Until I figure out what to do next."

It cooed at him from inside the bag.

He opened the door, leaned out, saw the maid hard at work in another room several doors down. He waited until he was sure she wasn't coming out right away before picking up the bag with the Special inside.

He rushed to Lisa's car, opened the passenger door, and set the bag gently on the front seat.

He returned to the room, pulled the Lisa burrito close to the door. Peeked out and watched for the maid again. She stood by her cart, retrieving some supplies. She was close enough that he could hear her singing Prince's "Let's Pretend We're Married" under her breath.

When she was out of sight again, he dragged Lisa to her Altima, opened the back door and shoved her inside.

He returned to his room, grabbed her purse. Locked up. Made sure the "DO NOT DISTURB" sign was secure upon the door handle. Lisa had ripped it but not enough to keep it from staying in place.

He got into her car, backed out, and headed for home.

For Chrissake, Jerry thought, *does it ever end?*

"It's like everybody in the world is trying their hardest to keep us from being together," he said to the thing in the passenger seat.

A big blue pickup truck waited for him in his driveway. In the back of the truck was the riding lawnmower Lisa had bought for his birthday. A guy with a long Willie Nelson ponytail stood on Jerry's front porch. He wore mirrored shades, held a clipboard in his hand. He waved as Jerry brought the Altima to a jerky stop. Jerry didn't wave back. He thumbed the remote on the sun visor to raise the garage door. Pushed another button to lower the passenger-side window.

"Help you?" he said.

"You're not supposed to be here," the man said.

"Excuse me?"

The man, whose name was DICK according to the nametag pinned to his shirt, looked down at his clipboard as he crossed the yard. "You're Jerry, right? Harford?"

"I know about the mower," Jerry said. "My wife couldn't keep a secret if her life depended on it."

Jerry drove into the garage, left the man standing there. The garage door rumbled down behind the Altima, the car's BREEZBYU vanity plate adding insult to injury (it had been his little joke when he first bought the car for Lisa, as he had always teased her about her habit of ignoring the speed limit, but she never got around to changing it).

Dick threw up his hands. *What's with this jerk?*

A minute or two later, Jerry stepped out through the front door.

"There you are," said Dick.

"Here I am," said Jerry.

"Is Mrs. Harford coming?"

"She's not," said Jerry. "She, uh...got wrapped up in something."

"I guess you'll have to sign for it, then." Dick held out his clipboard and pen.

Jerry scribbled his signature with one hand. Scratched himself through his pants with the other.

Dick noticed, scrunched up his nose. "Where, uh...where do you want it?"

"You can drop it right here."

Dick opened the truck's tailgate, positioned some boards to create a makeshift ramp. Jerry waited impatiently, his arms crossed in front of his chest. Occasionally he glanced toward the garage as Dick guided the mower down onto the lawn.

"You wanna step over here, pal, I'll give you a crash-course in what this baby has to offer," Dick said when that was done. "I just sprung for the same model myself, and I gotta tell y—"

"Not necessary," Jerry said. "We already bought it, so you can cut the friendly salesman act. I know how to drive a damn lawnmower."

"If you say so." Dick handed over the keys and the manual, looking like he wanted to say something a lot less polite.

Jerry watched him leave, then ran for the house.

He set the thing down in the tub. Ran some cool water over it until it began to purr again.

He perched himself on the toilet for a long time then, rubbing at his forehead.

After a while he looked down at his hands, saw Lisa's dried blood polka-dotting his wrists and knuckles.

"Jesus."

He turned on the bathwater. Kept it lukewarm, so as not to harm the Special.

As he tore off his clothes and eased into the tub with it, he saw that the rash had spread all the way

THE SPECIAL

up to his neck and nearly down to his knees. Random thumb-sized patches of the flush had started to turn a pale grayish-brown, the color of wet scabs. He ran his fingers over those spots and they blanched when he touched them. The skin contracted...like something alive, sentient, and fearful in the presence of a larger beast.

After he had scrubbed himself clean and the last of Lisa's blood had disappeared down the drain, Jerry went into the kitchen, where he threw open drawers until he found a box of aluminum foil. Another quick search turned up a roll of masking tape.

He proceeded to unroll the foil over the windows in the master bedroom, securing it in place with the tape.

Before long, the room was black. He could barely see his hands in front of his face.

He got some candles from the nightstand. Lit a few. Their flickering orange glow pushed back the shadows and filled the air with the scent of lavender. Jerry never would have admitted it to anyone, but he had always been a sucker for romanticism.

He set his watch before climbing into bed with the Special.

The thing pulsed against him, as if hungry for his touch.

He stroked it. Kissed it. Spent the next few hours with it.

But when his watched beeped 7:37, alerting him that the sun had set, he knew he had work to do.

He buried his wife's body beneath her beloved African tulip tree.

The night was cool. The moon was bright, but remained hidden behind a cluster of clouds as if respectful of the privacy Jerry needed for his task. It took him a little over an hour. He paused only to wipe sweat from his brow and, every now and then, to scratch at himself beneath his shirt and slacks.

At one point his fingertips came away wet with pus. His boxers felt damp; he was pretty sure he was starting to bleed down there.

He told himself that it would all be better as soon as he could get back to the Special.

The Special made everything okay.

Mort's Hole-In-the-Wall was all but deserted tonight, which was fine with Mike. He sat in his usual spot, sipping at his second rum-and-coke. Mort didn't seem to mind either. The bartender was busy trying to figure out how to work his new cash register; judging from the barrage of four-letter words that came out of him every few minutes he was already regretting the purchase. The joint's only other customers were a twenty-something couple necking in a dark corner at the back of the room.

The fat man finally gave up on the contraption. He waddled over toward Mike, started wiping down the bar with a rag. Tonight he wore a T-shirt that advertised "MOUSTACHE RIDES: FREE FOR ONE NIGHT ONLY."

"So, where's your buddy? Out with his better half again?"

"He's been sick," said Mike. "I don't think Jerry's doing too well, Mort. But then...I wouldn't really know. I haven't seen him."

Mike tipped back his glass to finish his drink. As he did so, he glanced up at the TV. His eyes grew wide.

Ivan's bearded face filled the screen. He was standing in front of Madame Zhora's place, beneath the bright light of a news camera. His bald head was shiny with sweat. The ticker beneath him read "RUSSIAN TRANSPLANT, 79, VICTIM OF VIOLENT CRIME."

"Hey, Mort, would you mind turning that up?"

Mort didn't mind.

"—for the person who did this," the big man was saying. "I know what is happening to you. I can help. In fact, I am the only one who can help you. I am here, *strashnyy*. And I am waiting. You do not know what you h—"

Behind Mike, one of the young lovers in the corner staggered over to the jukebox. He fed a dollar bill into the machine, and the opening chords of "Interstate Love Song" by the Stone Temple Pilots rattled every window in the joint.

"Son-of-a-bitch." Mort stomped out from behind the bar, pulled the cord out of the wall.

"Hey, man," said the music fan, "what's the big idea?"

Mort stuck his finger in the guy's chest, said, "My man over here is trying to watch the news. You got a problem with it, take your business somewhere else."

The guy puffed up his shoulders. Thought better of it. Returned to his table with his date.

"Thanks, Mort," Mike said, without looking away from the television.

"Don't mention it."

By now the scene had cut to a pretty blond reporter, who was clearly bewildered by her interviewee's cryptic comments. She stepped aside to give viewers a full view of the house. It was dark, like a person in mourning. She said, "Mr. Marovich's employer, a palm reader known as Madame Zhora, died earlier today from wounds the senior citizen suffered during a break-in earlier this week. Police say they are investigating several leads in hopes of apprehending the perpetrator as soon as possible. More on this story as it develops."

"You've look like you've seen a ghost, Mikey," Mort said. "You know that guy or something?"

But Mike's stool was empty. The only sign that he had ever been there were three five-dollar bills on the bar.

Mike parked by the curb several houses down from Jerry's place.

A yellow taxicab sat in the Harfords' driveway. A cloud of bluish exhaust billowed out from behind it.

"What are you up to, Jerry?" Mike whispered.

A minute or two later, Jerry emerged from the house. He got into the cab. It backed out and drove away.

Mike followed it.

The cab's destination: a place called the Sunrise Motel.

Jerry got out, swinging a key fob around one finger like a man without a care in the world. The cab drove away. Jerry entered one of the rooms.

Mike pulled into a gas station across the street.

He waited. Ten minutes passed. Fifteen. Jerry didn't come out.

Guilt consumed Mike's soul. Although he had never suggested that his friend carry on some sordid affair in a fleabag motel on the bad side of town...Jerry had been right, that day in the office. This was all his fault.

Mike put the car in gear. He knew what he had to do. It was time to come clean with Lisa.

———

This time he parked directly in front of Jerry's house.

He got out, rang the doorbell. Knocked. When no one answered he crept around to the side of the house.

From somewhere on the other side of town a police siren briefly wailed out like something dying, before fading into the distance.

As quietly as possible, Mike moved aside a propane grill to get to the door that led into the garage. He was surprised to find the door unlocked.

He turned on the light. Walked around Lisa's Altima and peered through its passenger-side rear window. The car was empty except for her purse, lying on its side, some of its contents spilled across the backseat.

He tripped over a shovel. It clanged against the

concrete. His heart thudding in his chest, he propped the shovel back against the wall—he noticed there was dirt caked on its blade, as if it had been used recently—and took a moment to regain his composure.

He opened the door into the house then, stepped into a kitchen lit only by a dim light over the stove. The room smelled of onions. An enormous stainless-steel refrigerator hummed to his left. On the fridge, held in place by a LAKESHORE SECURITIES magnet, was a photo of the Harfords during happier times. They stood arm in arm beneath a shaggy Bigfoot statue, making goofy faces.

"Hello?" Mike called out. "Lisa? Anybody home?"

Slowly, he made his way through the house, calling out her name every few steps, turning on lights as he went (somehow that made him feel less like an intruder)...until he came to the bedroom.

"Hello?"

He flicked on the light. Saw the foil covering every window. "What the hell is this?"

From the bathroom, he heard a squishing sound. Like a bare foot plunging into a puddle of mud.

After he was done checking out at the motel, Jerry made sure to drive at least ten miles from home before he pulled into the parking lot of a strip mall off the interstate.

He killed the Saab's headlights, drove around back.

He dropped the ripped-up pieces of his motel

bill, the bolt cutters, the pieces of the destroyed padlock, and the empty black box into one of the dumpsters, ignoring the "NOT FOR PUBLIC USE" signs posted everywhere.

He hurried back to the car. Froze in mid-step. Was he forgetting something?

Had the little "STICK IT IN HERE" label been missing from the side of the box? For that matter, when was the last time he had noticed it? It wasn't like he needed the instruction anymore.

He couldn't recall. Didn't plan on digging through the garbage to find out.

He wiped his hands on his pants, climbed back into his car. "Fuck it."

That made him laugh out loud.

He couldn't wait to get home and do exactly that.

———

Mike opened the bathroom door. Hit the light switch.

From behind the shower curtain, something squealed. An image of a piglet being slaughtered flashed through his mind, sending a chill down his spine.

He turned the light off. The squealing stopped.

He stepped into the room. Slowly pulled aside the shower curtain.

"Holy God in Heaven."

It made the squishing sound again. Its flesh seemed to ripple, as if scolding him for being here. Or perhaps for invoking God's name.

Mike tasted bile in the back of his throat. "What is this?"

On the other side of the house, he heard the garage door opening.

They nearly collided with one another in the kitchen. "Jerry," Mike said. "I can explain, man."

"Fancy meeting you here," Jerry said.

Mike recoiled as he saw what had become of his friend. A hideous pink rash covered the other man's wrists and hands. It was visible beneath his collar as well, creeping up his neck in wormy tendrils. The skin around his fingernails was bleeding. His lips were cracked and blue. And was he starting to lose his hair?

"Jesus Christ, Jerry. What's happened to you, man?"

"This?" said Jerry. He scratched at his cheek, leaving behind bruise-colored stripes across his flesh. "Oh, it's just a little rash. The doctor gave me some ointment for it. I'll be fine in ten days. Maybe more."

"It's because of that...thing, isn't it?" Mike said, his voice cracking. "The thing in your tub. It's from the box. You stole it. You brought it here, and it's changing you."

"Mike," Jerry said, "are you okay? Maybe you should stay away from Mort's for a while. I'm worried you might have a drinking problem."

"This must be what he was talking about. He said he knew what was happening to you. He said he could help."

"What are you talking about?" A desperate look flashed across Jerry's face, there and gone. "Who said he could help?"

"The Russian. Ivan. The guy who worked for

Madame Zhora. He was on the news. He said he had a message for whoever killed the old woman. He said he could help you. That thing must have gotten into your blood. You used it too much. You need help, Jerry. Maybe this Ivan guy has some kind of gypsy remedy, something from the homeland, I don't know—"

Jerry gave a snort of mocking laughter. "'Some kind of gypsy remedy?' 'Something from the homeland?'"

"Was it you?" Mike asked him. "Did you hurt her?"

"If you saw what's in the tub," said Jerry, "I think you know the answer to that question. What I wanna know is...how the hell did you get in my house?"

"The door was open. For God's sake, listen to me—"

"You think you can just walk into my house like you own the fucking place?"

"I came to help you, Jerry," Mike lied.

"I think it's a little late for that, don't you?" Jerry laughed, but there was something wrong with the sound of it. Somehow his raspy chuckle sounded like that thing, squishing in the tub.

"Jerry," Mike said. "Where's Lisa? Is she safe?"

Jerry scratched at his cheek again. "She got in the way."

"What do you mean, she got in the way? Got in the way of what?"

"Of me...and her."

"I'm calling the police," said Mike.

He started toward the phone. Jerry grabbed it first. He ripped it from the wall.

Mike scrabbled to find his cellphone in his pocket.

Jerry lunged for the knife rack on the counter. Whipped out a large butcher knife. He whirled toward Mike, sliced at the air with the blade.

Mike dropped his phone. "Jerry, calm down. Think about what you're doing—"

"Look," Jerry said, kneading at his crotch with his free hand. "Since you're my friend, I'll make this easy for you. You keep your mouth shut, you can use her whenever you want. I won't even charge you."

"Jerry, put the knife down!"

"Don't you remember how good she feels? Best sex you've ever had. That's what you told me. I didn't believe you. But, my God, you were right. I've never been happier. Come back to the bedroom with me, Mike. We can do her together. It's not queer if we don't touch each other."

"Jesus—"

"What do you say, man? She won't mind. I won't either.

That's what buddies do. They share."

"No, Jerry. I can't—"

"Fine. Have it your way."

Jerry leapt at him, slashing down with the knife. The blade caught Mike across the forearm. He screamed, clutched at the wound. Jerry swung the blade again, this time slicing Mike's cheek wide open.

Mike tried to hold his face together as Jerry kicked him to the ground.

Jerry leapt upon his back. Lifted the knife and brought it down. Lifted it and brought it down. Over and over and over...

...until, at last, Mike went limp.

Jerry stood with a groan and stumbled out of the kitchen.

He pulled back the shower curtain. "My poor baby. That bad man didn't hurt you, did he?"

He bent over, stroked the thing.

It purred louder than ever, undulating beneath his touch. He carried it into the bedroom.

He stepped out of the shower the next morning and stared at himself in the mirror.

The rash covered his entire body now. In places his skin had started to split open like overripe fruit: beneath his armpits, around his nipples, on the underside of his dick. His scrotum had become one massive, pus-filled blister.

He had to admit he looked pretty disgusting. But then, he had no one to impress but the Special. And the Special did not judge.

He spoke to her from the bathroom while he finished getting ready for work.

"I'm sorry, but I've got to go. If I don't, they'll get suspicious."

He coughed, spat a tooth into the bathroom sink.

Once he was dressed he went to stand over his lover in the dark bedroom. "Don't be like that. Of course I'll miss you. But this is the only way."

He leaned down, gave her a kiss.

"I'll be home by five-fifteen, I promise."

On his way out, he stepped over Mike's corpse in the kitchen and thought, *There was something I needed to take care of today....*

The guard looked up from a magazine he was reading. He frowned.

"Mister Harford? What are you doing here?"

"There's work to do, Earl," Jerry replied. "Always work to do."

"On a Saturday? That's harsh. You should be out golfing."

"Don't I know it." Jerry's finger hovered an inch from the elevator button. "Waitaminute. Today's Saturday?"

"Now I know you're pulling my leg," said Earl.

Jerry checked his cellphone. "I'll be damned. It is Saturday."

"You mean you really didn't know?"

"I'll be damned," Jerry said again.

"You okay, Mr. Harford?" Earl said. "You don't look too good."

Jerry left without another word.

The guard noticed he was walking with a limp, and when he pushed through the front door—which the custodial service had Windexed less than an hour ago—Mr. Harford's hand left a slimy print on the glass.

Earl shrugged, said, "Not my problem."

Their lovemaking was interrupted that evening by the sound of the doorbell.

Jerry tried to ignore it, hoping his visitor would assume no one was home after a minute and would go bother someone else. But when the bell chimed again, he knew he had no choice but to answer it.

He withdrew from the Special and threw on his bathrobe, moving slower than normal.

"I swear to God," he fumed, "if it's some brat selling Girl Scout Cookies. "

"Surprise!" exclaimed the group of people huddled on his front porch, as soon as he opened the front door.

They were old friends of his and Lisa's: John and Mandy Mulcrone, George and Cathy Peterson, and Kim Harwood from the house next door. Between them they carried a number of pastel-colored gift bags, a case of Jerry's favorite imported beer, and an expensive-looking bottle of wine.

"Here we are!" said the Petersons. "Ready to par-tayyy!" Their expressions changed from mirth to confusion, however, when they saw that Jerry was clad only in his dirty bathrobe.

"Where's that pretty wife of yours?" said Mandy, holding up the bottle of wine. "We've got some drinking to do!" As always, Mandy wore too much make-up in an attempt to look twenty years younger. She was also very proud of the boob job her husband had bought for her last summer. Jerry thought they looked ridiculous.

"Heya, Jerrrrry." Kim covered her mouth to stifle a belch. From the looks of it, she had started the party early. Jerry thought the young divorcee from across the street was sexy as hell, and he had fantasized about her more than once, but Kim never failed to make a fool of herself whenever there was alcohol involved.

They tried to come in, but Jerry blocked their way. He scratched his ass through his robe, squinted in the evening sunlight. The day was slowly dying, but the bright light hurt his eyes all the same.

"Jerry, my man. What's going on?" John offered his hand for a shake. He was a tall, muscular man with a heavy tan who jogged ten miles a day every day. His repertoire of off-color (and sometimes slightly racist) jokes was quite impressive, and he had one for every occasion. But Jerry got tired of constantly being pressured to go to the gym with him.

Jerry stared down at the other man's hand as if it were something that might bite him if he got too close.

His guests all looked at each other. The women whispered among themselves.

George cleared his throat, said, "We're, uh, here for your birthday bash?" George coached football at the local middle school. He even looked like a young John Madden. Jerry thought he was a loud-mouthed braggart, but his wife was good friends with Lisa so he had always done his best to tolerate the older man.

"My...um...what?" said Jerry.

"It's your birthday," Mandy said. "Unless you've decided you don't want to celebrate them anymore. Can't say I'd blame you at this point!"

"You're officially over the hill!" Cathy giggled. She was a Social Studies teacher at the same school where her husband coached football. She spoke with a hint of a British accent. She was a chubby lady whose sweet demeanor endeared her to everyone who met her, but with it came a childish, high-pitched laugh that grated on Jerry's nerves.

"The big four-oh!" Kim hiccupped.

Jerry said, "Today's my birthday?"

"You're kidding, right?" John said. "You seriously forgot your own birthday?"

"N-No," Jerry said. "Of course not. I'm just...I've been feeling a little under the weather, that's all."

"Oh, you poor thing," said Cathy.

Mandy gasped, held one perfectly-manicured hand to her bosom. "Oh, my goodness," she said. "We did arrive a little early. We didn't catch you two lovebirds in the middle of something naughty, did we?"

The others laughed.

"Nothing like that," Jerry replied. "Lisa's sick too."

"Can we see her?" Cathy asked. "I've got this new casserole recipe we need to discuss, it is positively scrumpt—"

"No!" Jerry said. "Lisa's...sleeping. I'm sorry she didn't call to let you know that we needed to cancel. Now you know. You have to leave now."

"Nonsense," said John. "We've been looking forward to this all week."

"I said to get out of here!" Jerry snapped at them. They all backed up, startled by his outburst.

Kim nearly fell off the front step, but Cathy caught her just in time. "You don't have to yell. God."

"Yeah," said George. "I thought Lisa was sleeping."

"Not anymore," said Jerry, "thanks to you."

"I'm not the one shouting," said George.

"Oh, piss off, Peterson!" Jerry said. "I never liked you anyway. Smug fuck. All of you, just get out the hell out of here and leave me alone. I told you I'm sick!"

"I'll say," Cathy mumbled.

"What's gotten into you, Jerry?" said John.

"Forget it," George said. "Let's go. To hell with this unappreciative prick."

"Yeah," said Mandy, grabbing her husband's arm. "We can go to our place and drink his present."

"Good idea," said Kim.

"Tell Lisa to call me when she wakes up, please?" said Cathy.

"Maybe," said Jerry.

He stepped back to close the door. His robe fell open. "Mother of God!" John said, covering his mouth.

Someone made a retching noise.

"Don't let him touch you," Jerry heard George say, just before he slammed the door in their faces. "That shit looks contagious. "

He climbed back into bed. Reached for the thing...

...only to discover that it had gone limp. Like a deflated basketball. Its color had faded once again to a pale blue. It had no pulse.

Jerry clutched it to his chest. Pleaded with it to wake up. But the thing flopped over in his hands like jelly.

He held it in his lap and started to sob.

He stumbled out of his car, wearing nothing but his bathrobe and a pair of Lisa's bedroom slippers.

In one hand he held a black plastic garbage bag; his other pounded desperately upon the front door, leaving smears of blood and pus upon the wood.

After a moment the curtain moved aside and Ivan peered through the glass at him.

"Let me in!" said Jerry. "Please."

The Russian smiled from behind his big red beard. "I see you got my message, *ubiytsa*."

The sound of locks snapping back.

The door opened and Jerry stumbled inside.

"Did you mean what you said? You can help me?"

"I can," Ivan said. "But first I must ask. The thing that you took from us. Is dead, no?"

Jerry glanced down at the bag in his hands. His eyes were wet with tears. "I think it is. Can you fix it?"

Ivan took the bag from him, said, "Come with me."

He led Jerry through the bead curtain. Up the stairs. He opened the door to the bedroom where Jerry had first encountered the Special. He turned on the light.

"You will rest for now. I will see what can be done about our friend here."

Jerry hesitated. Nodded. Didn't want to let the Special out of his sight, but knew this man was his only hope. "Y-Yeah. Okay."

Ivan turned to leave.

"For what it's worth," Jerry said, "I'm sorry."

Ivan stopped in the doorway, but did not turn to face him. "I understand," he said. "Too much is not enough." He held up the plastic bag. "Is not first time I have seen Special make men do crazy things."

"What about me?" Jerry said, opening his bathrobe. "Can you make this go away?"

He started scratching again. One of his nipples sloughed off, leaving a meaty hole in his chest. The wrinkly flesh of his abdomen contracted then went loose, contracted then went loose, like scrotum-skin during the moment of climax. He could feel it constantly moving, like something with a mind of its own.

"Will take care of you soon," Ivan said. "Better if you rest for now."

Jerry climbed onto the sagging bed.

The big man closed the door and locked it from the other side.

———

Ivan stepped through the basement doorway and into his workshop. He pulled the chain that dangled from a bare bulb in the ceiling, bathing the room in bright light. He turned on an oscillating fan in the corner of the room, wafting up the smell of sawdust, before approaching his workbench with heavy footsteps. The bench was painted school bus-yellow. Atop the bench sat a table saw, and on the wall behind it various tools hung on a shadow board: hammers, wrenches, screwdrivers, and a pair of mid-sized bolt-cutters. Taped to the adjacent wall was a poster of a pin-up girl lounging in a bubble bath in front of a hammer-and sickle background. On a little shelf beneath the poster sat a miniature boombox.

Ivan thunked the garbage bag down on top of his workbench, reached inside and gave the dead thing a squeeze.

He shook his head. "I cannot fix. *Vy dolzhny byt' zameneny*. I am sorry."

He dropped the bag into a nearby garbage can.

"So now we go to work. And this time, Ivan gets paid enough because Ivan is boss."

He chuckled to himself, a sound like thunder rumbling on the horizon, as he slid several bare pinewood planks from beneath the workbench.

He slipped on a dusty pair of goggles. Pushed the PLAY button on the mini boombox. The satanic stylings of Siberian black metal blared out from its speakers.

Then he started up the table saw, and it drowned out everything else.

———

Upstairs, Jerry thrashed about on the bed.

His body was changing faster now, minute by minute....

———

First, the Russian cut the planks of pine into seven one-foot squares, using the table saw, a tape measure, and a stubby carpenter's pencil.

He wiped sweat from his brow, flung it away. Working quickly but meticulously: *Izmeryat' dvazhdy, vyrezat' odin raz.* Measure twice, cut once....

He attached a jagged hole-saw bit to a cordless drill and bored a perfect round hole about twice the size of a golf ball into one of the squares.

He fit the five pieces together then with wood glue and screws, using an old T-shirt to clean up the stray glue that dripped onto his workbench in ropy brown strands.

Before him now, ahead of schedule, sat a cube-shaped box with no lid.

He fastened hinges to a sixth piece of wood, attached it to the top of the box.

He attached a hasp onto the front of the lid.

Stood back to admire his work. Nodded to the music for a moment and wiped more sweat from his brow.

Next he painted the box, turning the outside as

black as night. He used a hairdryer to dry the paint. Gave it a matte lacquer finish. Dried it.

Once that was done, he rummaged through a drawer until he found his handheld label-maker.

He fed a green strip of plastic into the label-maker. Adjusted the dial. Squeezed the handle. Adjusted the dial. Squeezed the handle. Taking his time with it, as his giant hands didn't make the job easy.

Four words. Thirteen letters, three spaces.

S...T...I...C...K....

He was starting on the last word when he heard Jerry's strangled scream from upstairs.

Ivan looked up with sawdust in his beard. He smiled.

Jerry scratched furiously at his scalp, came away with clumps of bloody hair sticking to his hands.

He rolled off of the bed and crashed to the floor on his hands and knees, gasping in pain.

Something tumbled out of his mouth. Six of his front teeth. He coughed and more fell out. His tongue whipped back and forth like something with a mind of its own. It probed, pushed, forced the last of his teeth from his skull.

And then it joined them. His tongue, bloated and gray, wiggled from between his lips and plopped onto the carpet like a dying leech.

Oh, God...what's happening to me?!

Jerry crawled to the door. Reached for the knob. Discovered it was locked.

He pounded on the door with his palms, as he could no longer close his hands into fists. His fingers were fused together now, like the webbed appendages of some amphibious beast.

Something milky-white, like semen, leaked from his eyes and nose and mouth.

He rolled over, onto his back, and his limbs curled into his body like those of a dying spider.

"P-Pease," Jerry wheezed, in a voice that had become like wet sand gurgling through a garden hose. "Pease...hep me."

Before long, the only sound that came out of him was a sick squelching noise.

Jerry's transformed body convulsed as if he were being electrocuted.

The swelling accelerated, faster and faster, until his features collapsed in upon themselves and his eyes and nose were sealed completely shut. His head no longer resembled anything remotely human, save for the aghast black "O" that had once been his mouth.

At last Jerry Harford lay still.

The lock on the door snapped back and Ivan entered the room carrying a low, trapezoid-shaped end-table. He positioned the table at the foot of the bed. Secured the box to the tabletop using brackets and wood screws.

Satisfied that his work was good, the Russian slipped his tools into his pocket.

He bent over Jerry's body then. Placed one foot on his chest.

He gripped the dead man's head between his hands and pulled.

Jerry's head separated from his body with a

sound like a corncob breaking in half. It was a bloodless affair.

Ivan lowered the head into the new box. Lined up the mouth with the hole.

Closed the lid and padlocked it tight.

He patted the top of the box with one hand before turning to leave the room.

Ne zakonchen. Almost forgot something....

He approached the box again. Dug deep into his pocket and pulled out a green strip of plastic. He tore off the backing paper, centered the label above the hole and pressed down on it with both thumbs.

Ideal'no. Perfect....

He picked up the headless body and dragged it out of the room.

He turned off the light. Closed the door and locked it with the key around his neck.

———

The neon "PSYCHIC" sign buzzed to life, flashing its eerie green glow upon the lawn.

A few seconds later, the battered piece of cardboard in the other window ("CLOSED UNTIL FURTHER NOTICE") was pulled away, and replaced by a brand new sign...fluorescent orange letters on a sin-black background painted neatly on a square piece of wood:

**UNDER
NEW
MANAGEMENT**

ABOUT THE AUTHORS

James Newman's published work includes the novels *Midnight Rain*, *The Wicked*, *Animosity*, *Ugly As Sin*, the collection *People Are Strange*, and the fan-favorite novella *Odd Man Out*. Next up are two more collaborations, *Dog Days O' Summer* and *Scapegoat* (with Mark Allan Gunnells and Adam Howe, respectively).

Mark Steensland self-published his first book while in fourth grade and has been telling stories ever since—some of them true. He became a professional journalist in high school, writing about movies for such magazines as *Millimeter*, *American Cinematographer*, and *Prevue*. His award-winning films (including *Peekers* and *The Ugly File*) have played in festivals around the world. His first novel —*Behind the Bookcase*—was published in 2012 by Random House. He most recently wrote *Jakob's Wife*, starring Barbara Crampton.